For Gay Bridgewood — it would be rude not to. J.W.

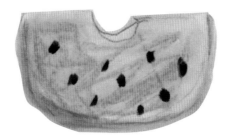

First published in Great Britain in 2006 by Andersen Press Ltd., 20 Vauxhall Bridge Road, London SW1V 2SA.
Published in Australia by Random House Australia Pty., 20 Alfred Street, Milsons Point, Sydney, NSW 2061.

10   9   8   7   6   5   4   3   2   1

British Library Cataloguing in Publication Data available.

ISBN-10: 1 84270 278 5
ISBN-13: 978 1 84270 278 9

The Really RUDE Rhino

Jeanne Willis and Tony Ross

Andersen Press
London

Once upon a time, there was a Really Rude Rhino.
He was rude from the day he was born.
"What a sweet little baby!" said his auntie.

"ₚₜₕhhhhhhhh!" went the Rhino.
"Don't be rude!" said his mother.

But the Really Rude Rhino took no notice.
He was rude to his brother.
He was rude to his sister.
He was even rude to his grandma.
"Give us a kiss," she said.

"Pthhhhhhhhh!"
went the Really Rude Rhino.

"He'll grow out of it," said his granddad.
But he didn't.
The Rhino was rude from dawn to dusk.
He was rude to his friends.
He was rude to his enemies.

He was even rude to the Queen.
"How do you do?" she said.

"Pthhhhhhhh!"
went the Really Rude Rhino.
"He'll grow out of it," said the King.
But he didn't.
The Rhino was rude from breakfast to dinner.

He was rude in public.
He was rude in private.
He was really, really rude to his teacher.
"See me after school!" the teacher said.

"ᴘthhhhhhhh!"
went the Really Rude Rhino.

"He'll grow out of it," said the dinner lady.
But he didn't.
The Rhino was rude from Monday to Sunday.
He was rude on holiday.
He was rude on sports day.

He was even rude on Christmas Day.
"What would you like for Christmas?" asked Santa.

"ᴘᴛhhhhhhhh!"
went the Really Rude Rhino.

He was so rude, his mother took him to the doctor.
"Open wide and say 'Ahh!'" said the doctor.

"Pthhhhhhhh!"

went the Really Rude Rhino.
"Will he ever grow out of it?" asked his mother.
"He's got Ruditis Rhinoceritis," said the doctor.
"There's no cure."

But there was.
Just after his fifth birthday, the Rhino woke up
in a particularly rude mood and decided to go out
all by himself because he was a big boy now.
"Whatever you do, don't go down to the
waterhole,"
said his mother.

"ᴘthhhhhhhh!"

went the Really Rude Rhino. And off he went.

Down by the waterhole, there was a little girl eating a slice of melon very politely.

The polite little girl couldn't see the Rhino, but
he could see her.
He was thinking how wonderfully rude it would be
to charge out of the bushes and make her run away
so he could eat the melon.
He lowered his horn. He stamped his feet and he

chaaaaaaaaaarged!

"ᴘthhhhhhhh!"
went the little girl.

"ᴡAAAAAAAAGH!"
went the Rhino.

He was so shocked,
he ran all the way home . . .

and he was never rude to anyone ever again.

Other titles written by Jeanne Willis
and illustrated by Tony Ross:

Don't Let Go!

I Hate School

I Want To Be A Cowgirl

Killer Gorilla

Manky Monkey

Misery Moo

Shhh!

Sloth's Shoes

Tadpole's Promise
(Smarties Prize Winner)

Whal Did I Look Like When I Was A Baby?